Rainy Day Music

Published by Advance Publishers, L.C.
www.advance-publishers.com

Written by Ronald Kidd
Art layout by Brad McMahon
Art composition by sheena needham • ess design
Produced by Bumpy Slide Books

ISBN: 1-57973-068-X

Blue's Clues Discovery Series

Hi, there! It's raining today, and Blue and I are trying to decide what to do.

Pitter-patter, pitter-patter. I love the sound of rain on the windows. It kind of sounds like music, don't you think? What's that, Blue? Listen again? OK.

Pitter-patter. Dingdong. Rap rap rap.
Oh! The music is different now. Why don't
we follow the sounds
to see where they
are coming from?

The music is coming from the door. Look!
Magenta is here for a play date!

So what could have made those sounds? Oh!
The pitter-patter was the sound of the rain. The
dingdong was Magenta ringing the bell. And the
rap rap rap was Magenta knocking on the door!

Hey! Making music is something we can do
on a rainy day! Do you think there are other
things in our house that make music? Me, too!

What's that, Blue? You want to make a musical instrument? Well, what kind of instrument?

Oh! We'll play Blue's Clues to figure out
what musical instrument Blue wants to make.
Will you help us? You will? Cool!

Shake shake shake.

Hey! What's that? It sounds like some more homemade music. Look, it's Magenta. She brought a bag of popcorn to pop.

What's that? You see a clue? Oh! The popcorn kernels are a clue! Thanks! You're good at this!

Hey, I think I hear a different kind of music. Yeah! A splashing sound. What could it be? Let's follow the sound and see!

It's Slippery Soap! Hi, Slippery!
We're finding things to do on this rainy day.
Blue wants to make a musical instrument, and
Magenta brought some popcorn to pop.

Whoa! Hi, Steve! Hey, I know something we can do, too! Let's make a band and play music together! We can call ourselves the Squeaky Cleans!
Good idea, Slippery! I've always wanted to play in a band.

So what can we use to play music in our band? A rubber duck! Yeah! A rubber duck squeaks! We can have a rubber duck in our band!

Okay, do you see anything else that we could use to make music for our band?

Yeah! A wet sponge! A wet sponge goes squish. You are so smart! So far we have a rubber duck to squeak and a sponge to squish.

Hmmm . . . If I took two toothbrushes and hit them together, I wonder if they would make a clack sound. What do you think? Me, too!

Now you have something to play, Steve.

The toothbrushes can be in our band—and I'll play them! C'mon, let's make some music!

Let's see how our band sounds!

Squeak, squish, clack, clack, clack.
Wow! We sound great! Let's do it again!
Squeak, squish, clack, clack, clack.

Boy, all this instrument playing is making me hungry. What's that, Magenta? Good idea! Let's go into the kitchen and make the popcorn you brought!

What do you see? A clue? Where? Oh! The drumstick is our second clue. Great!

So what instrument do you think Blue wants
to make with popcorn kernels and a drumstick?
Yeah, I think we need to find our third clue.
Come on, it's popcorn time!

Hi, Mr. Salt and Mrs. Pepper! Would you like to help us make popcorn?

We would love to make popcorn!

Here, I will put the popcorn kernels in the microwave!

Wow, listen to that popping noise! The popcorn popping sounds kind of like a drum going pop, pop, pop. Cool! We've found music in just about every room!

Yum. Good popcorn! Thanks for bringing it over, Magenta!

Do you see a clue? Where? The plastic bottle! Good job! Wait a minute . . . we've got all three clues! You know what that means! It's time to go to our . . . Thinking Chair!

It's still raining outside, but inside we're having a great time! We're playing in our cool band, the Squeaky Cleans—now featuring Blue and her new maraca!

Wow, that music has a good beat! I think I'm going to dance like Mr. Salt and Paprika. Thanks for all your help today. So long!

BLUE'S SHAKE & RATTLE MARACA

You will need: popcorn kernels, a 16-ounce plastic bottle with cap, craft glue, crayons, and paper

1. Pour the popcorn kernels into the bottle. (Dried beans also work.)

2. Put the cap on the bottle.

3. Use crayons to color the paper.

4. Glue the paper around the bottle.

5. Let the glue dry.

6. Shake!